PSYBERMAGICK

Some Other Titles from Falcon Press

Peter J. Carroll
The Chaos Magick Audio CDs

Phil Hine
Condensed Chaos
Prime Chaos
The Pseudonomicon

Christopher S. Hyatt, Ph.D.
Undoing Yourself With Energized Meditation & Other Devices
Techniques for Undoing Yourself (CDs)
Radical Undoing: Complete Course for Undoing Yourself (DVDs)
Energized Hypnosis (non-book, CDs & DVDs)
To Lie Is Human: Not Getting Caught Is Divine
The Psychopath's Bible: For the Extreme Individual
Secrets of Western Tantra: The Sexuality of the Middle Path

Christopher S. Hyatt, Ph.D. with contributions by
Wm. S. Burroughs, Timothy Leary, Robert Anton Wilson et al.
Rebels & Devils: The Psychology of Liberation

Christopher S. Hyatt, Ph.D. & Antero Alli
A Modern Shaman's Guide to a Pregnant Universe

S. Jason Black and Christopher S. Hyatt, Ph.D.
Pacts With the Devil: A Chronicle of Sex, Blasphemy & Liberation
Urban Voodoo: A Beginner's Guide to Afro-Caribbean Magic

Antero Alli
Angel Tech: A Modern Shaman's Guide to Reality Selection
Angel Tech Talk (CDs)

Joseph Lisiewski, Ph.D.
Israel Regardie and the Philosopher's Stone
Ceremonial Magic and the Power of Evocation
Kabbalistic Cycles and the Mastery of Life
Kabbalistic Handbook for the Practicing Magician
Howlings from the Pit

Sorceress Cagliastro
Blood Sorcery Bible Volume 1: Rituals in Necromancy

Steven Heller, Ph.D. & Terry Lee Steele
Monsters & Magical Sticks: There's No Such Thing As Hypnosis?

Israel Regardie
The Golden Dawn Audio CDs
The World of Enochian Magic (CD)

**For up-to-the-minute information on prices and
availability, please visit our website at
http://originalfalcon.com**

PsyberMagick

Advanced Ideas in Chaos Magick

Peter J. Carroll

THE *Original* FALCON PRESS

TEMPE, ARIZONA, U.S.A.

International Standard Book Number: 978-1-935150-65-7
ISBN 978-1-61869-650-2 (mobi)
ISBN 978-1-61869-651-9 (epub)
Library of Congress Catalog Card Number: 96-68644

First Edition 1995
First Falcon Edition 1997
Revised Second Edition 2000
Third Printing 2007
Third Edition Expanded and Revised 2008

Internal artwork by S. Jason Black
Diagrams on pages 29 & 31 © Phil Hine,
Courtesy of Doug Grant

Cover by Isis Solaris

The paper used in this publication meets the minimum requirements of the American National Standard for Permanence of Paper for Printed Library Materials Z39.48-1984.

Address all inquiries to:
THE ORIGINAL FALCON PRESS
1753 East Broadway Road #101-277
Tempe, AZ 85282 U.S.A.
(or)
PO Box 3540
Silver Springs, NV 89429 U.S.A.

website: http://www.originalfalcon.com
email: info@originalfalcon.com

For The Pact

TABLE OF CONTENTS

Chapter 1

PSYBERMAGICK

Introduction

*An introduction to the Ipsissimus Thesis of Frater Stokast-
ikos $\sqrt{-1}°$ by ourselfs.*

Abandoning conventional literary format, we present a
terse and abrupt catalogue of notes, observations, provoca-
tions, spells and rituals, to challenge any aspiring magus
with the wit and daring to play with them.

In celebration of our discovery of six dimensions, and out
of respect for St. Aleister Crowley who pioneered the format we use here, we now adopt the conceit of spelling the
art and science of the magus as MAGICK

*Upgrades for this third edition of Psybermagick written
during Autumn 2008, appear intermittently within the text
in italicized form.*

*A decade of further researches has convinced us of the
necessity of including the fourth (curvature) dimensions of
space and time in the Hyperwarp model to resume gravity
into a description of quantum-magical reality.*

*Plus the hyperspheres which constitute this universe and all
the particles in it must vorticitate, but more of that
anon............*

Commentary 1

We celebrate the beginning of a period of silence and our retirement from the roles of Magus and Pontiff of Chaos with the release of this volume.

We wandered the world for a decade and more as an 'I' seeking the secret magick of 'being'. Then, upon the realization of the Legion of our Doing, clarity dawned. Mastery of the Temple, Wealth, Honours and Power then followed more or less effortlessly.

You do not have to sell your soul to succeed with off-white magick. You merely have to recognize the existence of your other seven.

Well, the period of silence seems to have come to an end after scarcely a decade and a half. Time enough to make and launch a second child, to get the business empire running more or less on autopilot, and to crack a few esoteric problems that had bothered us for half a lifetime.

We wrote this book as a sort of 'bye for now'; outlining the sort of research we intended to pursue in the interregnum, hence the spaces which now come in handy.

The Maybelogic Academy www.maybelogic.org tempted us back into the public fray and led us to found Arcanorium College www.arcanoriumcollege.com where some of the worlds finest wizards and apprentices meet to conspire against consensus reality.

Chapter 2

WHY MAGICK?

Irrationale

We find ourselfs incarnate in an awesomely vast post-modernist universe of accidental origin amongst semi-intelligent apes grasping for emotional gratifications, power, personal identity and answers to silly questions, whilst trading these commodities between themselves. Yet the recommended gratifications and socially-approved identities seem such dull travesties of what two whole kilograms of brain might achieve. Worse still, the apes' gods and Gods, for all their cosmic pretensions, appear as laughably-parochial anthropomorphisms, abstracted from faulty language structures, compounded by the pack-animal urge to obeisance.

Contemptuous of all the rubbish on sale, some attempt to create their own powers, gratifications, identities and explanations, and call themselfs magicians.

Hubris, then, accounts for the best of it:
But Why Not!

As belief in one's capabilities self-evidently leads to increasing capabilities, magicians consider it worthwhile to believe in their ability to accomplish the impossible, even if they only succeed at this occasionally.

Indeed, and although it hurt lots, we even learnt enough mathematics during the sabbatical to challenge the Big Bang Theory.

Commentary 2

As nothing has any meaning other than that which we choose to give it, we must either invest belief and meaning in something or abandon the game and go straight to oblivion.

In selecting beliefs, we might as well go for maximum entertainment value and capability enhancement, regardless of the so-called 'facts'; for if a human really wants something, statistics count for nothing.

Personally, we attribute much of our success to a generous contempt for the apparent facts which a science education inadvertently taught us.

Spot the treble entendre.

We doubt that any facts actually exist.

We only have observations and interpretations.

Most of the interpretations remain questionable.

Belief in any god enhances self-belief but at the price of all the theological nonsense that accompanies it. Why not then adopt belief in oneself directly as a magician?

If it occasionally fails them fall back upon

$Pm = P + (1-P) M^{1/P}$ *(2nd equation of magic, Liber Kaos).*

Belief Bends Probability (sometimes).

Chapter 3

OURSELFS

Multimind

Some philosophers and psychologists bemoan the disintegration or fragmentation of the self in the contemporary world.

We celebrate this development.

The belief in a single self stems from religious monotheisms having only a single god. Let us throw out the baby with the bath water.

If you consider yourself an 'individual', in the sense of 'indivisible', you have not lived.

If you merely consider yourself as a single being capable of playing various roles, then you have yet to play them *in extremis.*

The selfs must allow each self a shot at its goals in life, if you wish to achieve any sense of fulfillment and remain sane.

So many people seem to spend their lives trying to appear normal predictable and consistent to themselves and those that surround them. They just end up bored with themselves, bereft of any depth of inner resources, suffocated by the inhibitions that defend their own monolithic identities.

If you can only live once at a time you may as well have several parallel identities on the go at that time.

Commentary 3

The authors apologize in advance for any irritation and confusion caused by the use of standard Chaotic grammar which avoids all concepts of 'being', and uses 'we' instead of 'I', in recognition of the legionary nature of the personal multimind.

If you still do not accept the principle of multiple selfs then consider why humans spend so much time at the temples of Venus, Luna, Bacchus and Mars, trying to escape from their workaday Solar 1 selfs, in pursuit of love, sex, intoxication and violent entertainments.

We wouldn't change a word of that. Verily we conjure the convenient illusion of singular self to simplify our dealings with others and ourself(s).

In reality we have the name 'Legion', we have worlds and gods and demons partying within.

Loosen the bonds of Ego, and relax that tired old post-monotheist theory of mind to open the treasure house within.

Chapter 4

MAGICK I

Science & Magick

The following ten chapters augment the technical procedures and general theory of magick given in our two previous books *Liber Null & Psychonaut* and *Liber Kaos: The Psychonomicon.*

STOKASTIKOS'S LAW
"Any sufficiently advanced form of magick will appear indistinguishable from science."[1]

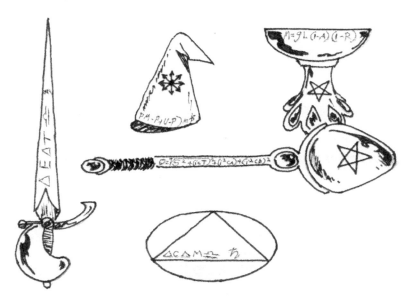

---

[1] Arthur C. Clark coined this statement in its obverse form.

Commentary 4

Our language structures impose causality as a mode of perception. Causality does not rule this universe. Humans label events which they associate together frequently as causally connected, and events which they associate together only occasionally as coincidence.

Personally, we prefer to consider science as the study and engineering of highly probable coincidences, such as the tendency of apples to fall downwards when dropped from trees. We prefer to consider magick as the study and engineering of less probable coincidences, such as the tendency of trees to drop apples when we ask them to.

Everything works by magick; science represents a small domain of magick where coincidences have a relatively high probability of occurrence.

Half of the skill in magick consists of identifying probabilities worth enhancing.

A few more equations have phenomenised during the interregnum,

$$\Delta SK^\circ \, \Delta t_3 \sim \hbar$$

Shows a new member of the class of Heisenberg style uncertainty/indeterminacy relationships where effects associated with minimal entropy can propagate across large distances in three dimensional time.

Chapter 5

MAGICK II

Magickal Attack

> Attack by Enchantment
> Defend by Evocation

Commentary 5

Remember (and use) the fact that imagined magickal attack creates far more casualties than actual magickal attack. However, do not risk trying to divine the nature of a real magickal attack, for this will increase your vulnerability to it.

For defence evoke or create a general purpose servitor/cybermorph/eidolon. Forget about such naïve procedures as erecting astral mirrors or shields: these have little other than psychological value. Attack or counterattack vigorously with properly ensigilized enchantments tailored to create highly specific effects. The bullet rather than the grenade.

Do unto others as they would do unto you, but do it first.

Such secrets we can reveal, having retired from active service after many campaigns

— *Field Magus Stokastikos*

Actually we seem to have taken up the baton several times since. The universe seems to fill up with fresh entropy malice and stupidity the minute you turn your back on it.

Humans fight mainly to change the behaviour of their rivals and adversaries. The best magical attack accomplishes this behaviour change directly and bypasses the intervening carnage entirely.

Chapter 6

MAGICK III

Wand or Cup?

Enchant Long
&
Divine Short

Commentary 6

Wand or Cup?

If only one fifth of your spells work you have real power.

If only one fifth of your divinations work you have a serious disability.

Spells cast well in advance can take advantage of the copious chaos in the interim, but that same chaos will tend to reduce divination to a shambles.

'Enchant Long and Divine Short.'

Yes indeed, engrave that in Enochian, Ouranian Barbaric and in the vernacular on your altar.

This supremely important dictum ranks alongside such universal items of wisdom as 'Don't Trust People In Suits' and 'Don't Eat Anything Bigger Than Your Head.'

Waste not your energies on considerations of fate and destiny, go forth and make the universe do what you want!

Chapter 7

MAGICK IV

Sacrifice

DON'T SACRIFICE, INVEST!

By sacrifice, the religious attempt to invest in spiritual agencies.

Magicians know better; they invest directly in themselfs, cutting out the middleman. Sacrifice only those things which get in the way of desire, not the thing itself.

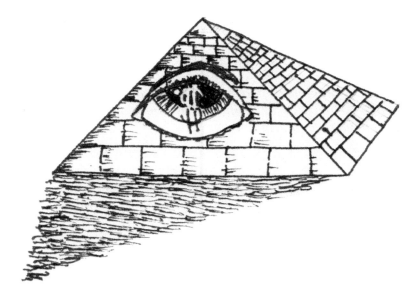

Commentary 7

Some neophytes imagine that you can conjure wealth by burning bank notes to the gods.

Never insult money or blaspheme it by gambling, unless you want to banish it.

If you want money, then sacrifice it only on opportunities which will make money. Treat money as a major God: for its capricious and awesome power rivals that of even love and war. Money acts as a vast, intelligent organism which lives by occupying part of the brain of nearly everyone on this planet. Mammon seems far more awake at this moment than many gods we could mention.

Have faith in the power of Money.

'I Love Money and Money Loves Me.'

Repeat continuously and preferably in an ensigilised language, to make it stick in the subconscious, during any wealth magic conjuration.

Bad investment = Blasphemy.

Never invest in any situation where you have no power to skew the odds in your favour by the exercise of effort, intelligence or parapsychology.

Chapter 8

MAGICK IV

Magickal Medicine

Paradox: If homeopaths knew how homeopathy actually worked, it wouldn't work.

Overstanding: Homeopathy works by Magick, i.e., the parapsychological effect of operator intent. Homeopaths have to believe in bogus theories to achieve real effects.

Commentary 8

The erroneous theories of homeopathy arose from the early, purely empirical, practices of immunisation, and an ignorance of Avogadro's number which quantifies the number of molecules in a given sample. An understanding of the mechanics of active and passive acquired immunity, which came much later, would have prevented the development of such theories in the first place.

Homeopathy has let magick back into medicine at the small price of demanding belief in a completely wrong theory by its practitioners.

Spell:—
Iatrogenic homeopathy apparently works well in black magick. The sorcerer antidotes the target with a potentization of itself. Perhaps we should not have mentioned this ...

Placebo and Nocebo medicine work quite astonishingly well if you look at the literature in this expanding field.

Physician's beliefs and intents often seem to cure in the absence of physiologically effective procedures.

Modern Alchemists never seen short of testimonials from grateful customers.

Chapter 9

MAGICK VI

The Fourth Equation of Magick[1]

Eidolonics

$$P_e = P + (1 - P)L^{\frac{1}{P}}$$

Where all factors lie on a scale of 0-1
and:—
Pe = the probability of accomplishing something by the use
   of an Eidolon.
P = the probability of the event occurring by chance alone.
L = the quality of the magical link.

---

[1] See our *Liber Kaos: The Psychonomicon* for the first three.

Commentary 9

THE EIDOLON EVOCATION

CONJURATION: —
Let the magickian fashion a Material Basis for a general purpose cybermorph, sparing no expense or skill. Let the magickian physically carry the material basis at all times close to the body. Let the magickian mentally carry the astral image of the material basis to the point of clear hallucination during any spare waking moment and, if possible, whilst dreaming. Let the magickian, by profound effort of ritual, phantasy and imagination, treat the eidolon's material and astral forms as sigils for a named semi-autonomous sentience.

The magickian will create a reusable multi-task servitor by such conjurations, for which the first equations factors take an optimum unitary value. Thus only the problem of a magickal link awaits solution in any particular spell of enchantment or divination at which the magickian directs the eidolon. Although the neophyte must learn the many and varied conjurations of the art and science, the master will usually prefer the greater speed and efficiency that an eidolon cybermorph offers.

We still don't believe in 'Spirits' in the traditional sense of the word, yet we have increasingly relied on handmade synthetic entities to accomplish difficult acts of probability manipulation or information retrieval. It takes far less time than making spells from scratch. Just pick up the groundsleve of an appropriate entity from the altar and visualize it going off to do the business. Simply Fire and Forget. Upgrade to modern magical missile technology.

Chapter 10

MAGICK VII

The Fifth Equation of Magick

$$0 = \sqrt{s^2 + (ict)^2 + (i^2ca)^2 + (i^2cb)^2}$$

Where:—
s = spatial separation
t = temporal separation (ordinary time)
a & b = temporal separation in two dimensions of imaginary time
$i = \sqrt{-1}$
c = lightspeed

Note that this equation gives the 'psispacetime' separation between events in a six-dimensional Pythagorean form. Non-local exchange of information can occur when psispacetime separation equals zero. Due to the large value of c, zero separations at terrestrial distances occur when:—

$$t \approx \sqrt{a^2 + b^2}$$

Commentary 10

Clearly, squaring out the i factors arising from modeling time as an imaginary form of space, and imaginary time as an imaginary form of imaginary space, yields the following simplification of the full form of the fifth equation set to a zero value:—

$$s^2 - (ct)^2 + (ca)^2 + (cb)^2 = 0$$

Quantum non-locality then appears as the limited case, where $a = b = 0$, and information passes instantaneously along lightcones.

Magick then appears as the more general case where:—

$$0 \neq \sqrt{a^2 + b^2}$$

Note that the fifth equation of magick models both space and time with the same dimensionality of three. Do not panic at your inability to see the other two dimensions of time, you cannot actually even see the first one. More of this later in the hyperwarp chapters.

Basically, because lightspeed has a very high value, you do not have to worry about spatial separation, at least on planetary scales, when attempting divination or enchantment. This may seem empirically obvious to practical magicians, but theoretical parapsychologists need explanations.

Chapter 11

MAGICK VIII

Null Path Enchantments in Six-Dimensional Psispacetime

The figure below shows the three dimensions of time with a circle of unit radius in the plane of ab.

Enchantments launched by a magickian at t_0 can act on the circle of probabilities at t_1 and may appear as changed conditions at t_2 when the magickian arrives at t_2.

Conversely, retroactive enchantments can have the odd effect of apparently altering t_{-1} properties, so long as these do not have the effect of preventing the enchantment. This can result in a change of conditions at t_0.

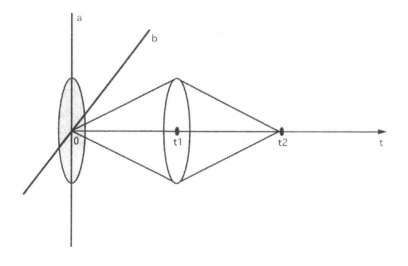

Commentary 11

Enchantments thus 'land' at a distance in the future twice as great as the radius of the circle of imaginary time probabilities with which they interact. Retroactive enchantment acts on a circle of probabilities at t_{-1}, not shown in the figure above, which then feed back to the present at t_0. As we can only observe the instant of the present in t, any debate about what 'really' occurred at t_{-1} becomes academic.

Note that the probability circle increases in size with time by a factor of πt. Thus, if tomorrow contains a million possibilities, the day after contains 3 million. Enchant long!

Note also that an observer at t_0 can in no way observe or interact with so-called 'parallel universes' represented by the shadowy circle in imaginary time at t_0. They may well exist, but they may as well not exist, if you see what we mean.

Retroactive enchantment can only occur if the enchantment does not alter the present in such a way that the enchantment no longer takes place.

Retroactive enchantment serves to enhance the probability of a particular past having contributed to the present, leading to the future going off in a somewhat unlikely direction.

Chapter 12

MAGICK IX

Null Divinations in Six-Dimensional Psispacetime

The figure below shows the three dimensions of time with circles of unit radius in the plane of *ab*.

Divinations performed by a magickian at t_0 to scry events at t_2 or t_{-2} can only succeed if the magickian can identify a dominant probability amongst the plethora of information in either circle. Only divinations which reveal unexpectedly high probabilities tend to count as successes.

Note that you can only scry the imaginary past of an event at t_2, not the event itself.[1,2]

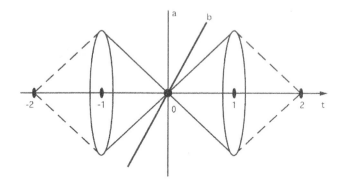

---

[1] *Note that you can only scry the imaginary future of t_{-2} as well.*

[2] *Note that the whole idea of past and future 'events' as phenomena that really did or really will occur remains a convention of speech, memory and expectation. From the standpoint of any moment of the present all pasts and futures have only a probability of occurrence.*

Commentary 12

The very act of 'looking' in divination can tend to distort the probability of what you look at. Divination can thus act as enchantment in a way quite beyond the mere effect of self-fulfilling prophecy in the ordinary sense.

Divination also becomes progressively more difficult with time, as circles of probability in imaginary time enlarge.

We have never met anyone who could consistently divine accurately; although a huge market exists for those who divine poorly or merely pretend to. Oddly, the market for those who can enchant reasonably well seems hardly to exist, probably because only those who cannot, regularly advertise, and those who can, use it more directly to their own advantage.

Perhaps the same applies to divination, but we doubt it, on account of the foregoing technical difficulties.

If in doubt, always attempt to force the hand of chance.

Chapter 13

MAGICK X

Retroactive Enchantment

Despite the ease with which this effect manifests in delayed choice quantum optics experiments, some magickians still seem to have difficulty in summoning the belief to make this work on the macroscopic scale.

Try this experiment:—

Wait until you have lost something.

Rather than conduct further fruitless searches, try and trick your subconscious into believing that you actually put the object in a particular place where you actually want to find it. If you have to, you can even use a location that you have already searched, but in this case you will also need to make your subconscious recollection of having searched that place as hazy as possible.

Then, whilst occupying your conscious mind with some powerful distraction (anger works well), go to the chosen location and retrieve the lost object.

Commentary 13

The subtle mental manoeuvres required for retroactive enchantment depend upon suspending conscious deliberation and memory, and will fail if you try thinking consciously about your thoughts.

Compare this kind of will-perception coordination with the hand-eye coordination of catching a ball. Both work best when performed automatically.

If you ever succeed with a trick like this, and you wish to retain and develop the ability without going mad, then we suggest that you do not seek alternative explanations. Accept instead the belief that the past has some mutability, or better still that no 'real' time past exists, but that the imaginary time past contains probabilities restricted only by the observed conditions of the present moment.

If you think that this sounds completely crazy and deranged then have a look at The Delayed Choice Quantum Eraser Experiment which reproduces the result quite reliably.

Chapter 14

POLITICS I

Chaocracy

It has taken us two million years to elevate politics from the level of a monkey squabble, to a level comprehensible to a six year old child.

Towards the end of the twentieth century, the question "What will succeed democracy?" seems as un-askable as the question, "What will succeed monotheism," would have seemed in the fourteenth century.

Can nobody contemplate any advance upon the least worst of all systems tried so far?

The Problem:—
1. We have to delegate responsibility for government, as most of us have better things to do for most of the time.
2. Nobody who wants political power should have it.
3. De-electable bodies retain power largely by maintaining the interests of the stasis quo, and cannot act with the impartial wisdom that the luxury of time to govern could allow them to develop.
4. Elected bodies abrogate much of their power to people who act as monarchs, and then waste much of their time and efforts in factional infighting.

Commentary 14

If we have any faith in the stochastic principles to which we owe our very reality and existence, then we should perhaps consider CHAOCRACY.

Let us select a legislative body by purely random means. Let us reward those so chosen with salaries which put them beyond corruption. Let us replace one half of those chosen by random means every few years.

A chaocracy will contain representative proportions of all ages and sexes.

A chaocracy will have the assistance of a civil service to advise it.

A chaocracy will free us from the conflict of party political ideology with conscience, and free us from the distasteful business of casting our votes amongst professional liars.

Let a chaocratic government debate openly but legislate by secret ballot.

Let the outcome of such vote act as the head of state rather than invest one person with this power.

We trust people's lives to randomly selected juries as the only fair method; should we use any less fair method for a nation or a planet?

The political class in Europe now seems hell bent on replacing Democracy with Synarchy, and they will probably succeed for a while. When the revolt finally happens, Chaocracy may eventually flower.

Chapter 15

POLITICS II

Conspiracy Theory

Nobody has unity of desire;
The selves within the person
Conspire to fulfill their instinctual agendas.
Such conspiracies spiral upward in fractal self-similarity
through domestic, social, workplace, national and interna-
tional scenarios, yielding chaotic outcomes at all levels.

Conspiracies exist all right:
But Fuckup mostly rules the outcome.

*An overdue and bloody revolution left the French with a
fear of Anarchy. Subsequent francophone esoterics tended
to center around middle class neo- Masonic initiatives
aimed at preserving social order with Synarchic principles.*

*Multiple French disasters in war only served to strengthen
this tendency. The absence of Crowleyesque initiative to
modernise French esoterics early in the 20th century, or an
occult revival in the post 1968 period has resulted in a late
19th century political metaphysic forming the philosophical
basis of European Union.*

Commentary 15

Conspiracy theory, like causality, works fantastically well as an explanatory model but only if you use it backwards. The fact that we cannot predict much about tomorrow strongly indicates that most of the explanations we develop about how something happened yesterday have (like history in general) a high bullshit content.

Three things feed conspiracy theories:—
Paranoia born of the need for self importance.
The need for enemies; which comes down to more or less the same thing.
The desire for belief even in malignant forms of control rather than in the reality of pure chance chaos and accident.

The Synarchist manifesto appears quite explicitly in the writings of the nineteenth century Martinist esotericist Yves Saint D'Alvedre and in all the European Union constitutional documents. Thus we can hardly describe it as a secret conspiracy. Neither should we feel excessively paranoid about it, for it too will pass after a period of hopeless inefficiency and survivable unpleasantness.

As population, ecological, climatic, and resource pressures rise over the coming decades we can expect to see more and more governments based on cabals of those who imagine they know our collective long term best interests but which act with scant regard for freedom of information or our opinions.

Chapter 16

POLITICS III

Conspiracy Practise

Any conspiracy lacking internal conspiracies will rule its world.

Only through absolute loyalty to each other can the few control the many.

Commentary 16

The extreme simplicity of these statements belies both their awesome applicability to conspiracies at all fractal levels and the virtual impossibility of their achievement.

In practise the power of any conspiracy rises and falls in inverse proportion to the power of its internal conspiracies.

Mutual guilt and bribery mainly hold together conspiracies whose ideologies command insufficient loyalty, but this makes them vulnerable.

Never join a conspiracy that you could possibly betray, because if you could, someone else will.

Most semi-secret societies have no secrets to protect except the embarrassing foolishness of their own practices.

Truly secret societies will usually have initiation practices which serve to incriminate applicants.

Chapter 17

POLITICS IV

Tetragrammaton of the Illuminati

LAWFUL

JEHOVIC   CHRISTIC

NASTY ——————————————— NICE

SATANIC   LUCIFERIC

CHAOTIC

LAW: TRADITION, ORDER, STASIS QUO
CHAOS: INNOVATION, NEOPHILIA
NICE: ALTRUISM (INCLUSIVE SELFISHNESS)
NASTY: NARROW (EXCLUSIVE SELFISHNESS)

Commentary 17

The Occult Technology of Power

The Jehovic programme of lawful nastiness dominates most psychopolitical systems from the nation state down the self-similar fractal ladder to the selfs within a person. Such systems tend to maintain their stasis quo at the expense of surrounding systems or sub-systems.

The Christic and Satanic programmes have little overall effect, as they expend themselves against the Jehovic programme and each other; and few systems manage to display either permanent beastliness or saintliness.

The Jehovic programme can readily manipulate and control both programmes to suit its own agenda; it can always use saints and criminals.

Only the Luciferic programme allows evolution, as the Illuminati well know. In recent centuries the dominant psychopolitical Jehovic forces have come to realize that a limited amount of Luciferic creative chaos can give them an edge over systems which do not possess it.

We aim to give them a great deal more than they bargained for.

Lawful Evil versus Chaotic Good, the never-ending story, the eternal fight.

Today's liberation becomes tomorrow's oppression.

So keep pushing the boundaries.

Chapter 18

POLITICS V

Liberty, Equality, Fraternity

How sweet, but sadly mistaken, our old formula sounds. Unfortunately, you have to discount fraternity, once numbers exceed the maximum cohesive pack size of about a hundred and fifty persons. This leaves equality at war with liberty.

Enforcing equality to compensate for the monstrous unfairness of nature destroys liberty.

But total liberty leads to various forms of 'aristocracy' and decay.

Yet total equality leads to oppressive forms of stateism and decay.

However, equality of opportunity leads to a vibrantly chaotic and creative meritocracy.

Commentary 18

Creeping stateism, governmental interference in every-thing, and the absurdity of 'parity' and equality of reward regardless of accomplishment, threaten the wealth and cre-ativity of every nation, and will abort any new renaissance in Europe if unchecked.

No left wing parties have any respect for liberal economic values; and most centre and right wing parties merely pro-mote a paternalistic stateism.

Does it thus fall to the self-reliant students of the ruggedly individualist philosophy of magick to champion a certain measured libertarianism?

We note that the last few decades of increasing equality of opportunity have led to a frighteningly efficient social sorting mechanism. We now have a world famous Under-class in the UK, untainted by the slightest upward mobility, for the upwardly mobile went elsewhere.

Walk the streets with caution.

Chapter 19

POLITICS VI

The Illuminati

In view of the foregoing theoretical considerations, the Illuminati changed their tactics sometime in the twentieth century, preferring to conspire against the stasis quo at all fractal levels simultaneously and to hide and generate the resources, information and occult technology used for this by dispersing it amongst many seemingly innocuous enterprises and even into enemy camps. Leaking conspiracies provide the best possible vehicles for disseminating both information and disinformation. The enhancement of the fuckup factor in any enemy conspiracy subverts it far more effectively than direct assault.

The Illuminati now structures itself amorphously, and does not react to attack, which would allow the enemy to structure the conflict. Rather it attacks in directions chosen at random and then runs away to fight another day. Many members of the Illuminati remain unknown to each other or unaware of their own membership.

Do you believe any of this?
Do you want to make it happen?

Well we live in hope. We win some and we lose some.

The evil Illuminati seem rather active in the field of religious fundamentalism at the time of writing, and democracy retreats in many areas.

Commentary 19

We Can Only Escape The Bloody And Ignorant Nightmare Of History By Exploring Alternatives Which Today Look Frighteningly Weird.

Immanentize The Eschaton
any which way you can
shun entropy
but exploit chaos to the full

We have much to do if we want a chaoist eschaton rather than an entropic one, a dreamtime fifth aeon rather than a nightmare one.

15 years on and things still look a bit grim. Religion has become more rabid; consumerism runs wild and fails to satisfy. Global ecological catastrophe threatens.

In many areas we seem to have got stuck in a mindset of 'Quantity over Quality.' The very failure of religion and consumerism often leads to the absurdist position of 'well we obviously need MORE of it then!' Many have become like miserable obesity cases trying to cheer themselves up with more food.

Junk food, junk religion, and junk products just leads to excessive numbers of junk people living junk lifestyles.

Science guided by the light of a Magical Panpsychic Neo-Pantheist philosophy seems like a better idea.[1]

---

[1] See *The Apophenion.*

Chapter 20

Heresy I

Spirituality

Magick will not free itself from occultism until we have strangled the last astrologer with the guts of the last spiritual master.

After decades of mounting anger at prevailing fashions in stupidity we present something to offend everyone in the following heresy chapters.

Never discard the negative roots of any equation; always look at the dark side of any enlightenment.

Commentary 20

Only contra-initiative absurdity commands belief. Never try to design a spirituality based on credible ideas. Start with something really idiotic. Denials of death and sex or magick often prove useful, for example. You can make yourself into a spiritual master very easily using the Goebbels'[1] technique. Find a handy lie and just keep repeating it loud and long enough until people believe you.

Language alone makes religion possible. The nonsense equation $2 + 2 = 5$ has the effect of a virus which will undo the entire edifice of mathematics if left uncorrected. The false linguistic equations underlying paradigms of spirituality have a similar effect on thought.

Exercise: Identify the erroneous linguistic equations which create the following ideas:—
The Supreme Being,
Higher Things,
Spiritual Values.

All plans for utopia lead straight to hell.

Rather we should plan for agreeable ongoing processes.

---

[1] Third Reich Minister of Propaganda.

Chapter 21

HERESY II

Predictions

1) Chemistry undid Personality.

2) Physics undid Determinacy.

3) Biology will soon undo most of our preconceptions about 'human beings'.

4) Memory modification will eventually undo the rest.

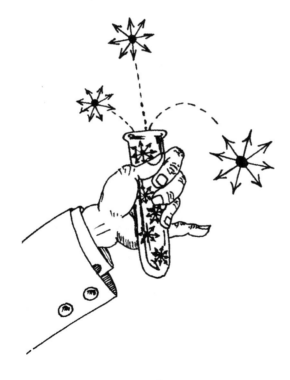

Commentary 21

1) Psychopharmacy reveals that personality depends entirely upon chemistry and thus consists entirely of chemistry. *In vino veritas* indeed. Chemicals can make you schizophrenic, ecstatic, depressed, extrovert, introvert, libidinous, celibate, aggressive or passive. So much for the notion of essential self.

2) Today does not completely determine tomorrow, much less next week. We have awoken to Chaos from Newton's sleep and single vision.

3) If intelligent aliens haven't shown up within a couple of decades, we will probably have made our own.

We now seem within spitting distance of making our own aliens from either meat or machinery.

4) Memory Defines Identity. Think about it, or if you can't, try reading Philip K. Dick.

We may not even need direct neural interfaces to rewrite memory. In my own lifetime I have seen the history books rewritten for sociopolitical purposes.

Chapter 22

HERESY III

Our Glorious Simian Heritage
Obeisance, obeisance, obeisance!
Offering your arse in submission
To the bull ape of the troop.
Kneeling before the chieftain;
Penance and sacrifice to the shaman;
Genuflection to the Lord;
Confession to the priest.
Prostration before the Almighty Ape
In the sky.

Commentary 22

The expectation that we shall receive reward and escape punishment by acts of submission, lies deep in our pack animal brains and contributes heavily to our hunger for spiritual masters and deities.

It also endears that other arse licking pack animal, the dog, to feeble-minded members of our own species.

Well that's what you get for incarnating as a member of a social species, a frightening suggestibility.

As you read this our words speak themselves inside your head.

Always consider the qualifications of anyone who assumes or professes authority, what do they really know?

Authorities on spirituality can rarely give a half coherent explanation of what they persuade us to believe they know.

They achieve authority by stage management and then exploit audience suggestibility. Same old trick they have pulled for thousands of years.

Chapter 23

HERESY IV

Elitism

Our ancient Celtic ancestors said: "Never give a sword to a man who cannot dance."

We might well add: "Never give a wand to anyone who cannot handle ordinary reality."

Magick will tend to amplify whatever tendencies a person has. It will increase general incompetence in life, just as readily as it will augment competence.

Although we have seen those who started off reasonably well-organized and made a magnificent success of their lives with magick, we have observed plenty of unpromising cases taking a powered nose-dive to disaster with occult assistance.

The casualty list has grown considerably since we wrote the above.

Magic doesn't suit everyone. Only those prepared to take full responsibility for themselves should apply.

The rest should find themselves the cheapest and most benign sources of outside guidance.

Commentary 23

The best orders and the best books on magick make the neophyte work very hard to gain anything. For, in brutal fact, nothing of any value comes from involving people who do not pursue excellence for its own sake in magick.

Magick does not offer an escape from ordinary reality: rather it offers a full-on confrontation with it, which one can easily lose.

When inexplicable or extraordinary things happen many people look for occult explanations and hidden meanings. For the rest of the time they think they know roughly how or even why ordinary things happen, and what remains impossible.

The magician turns this process on its head and regards 'ordinary reality' as extraordinary and perhaps ultimately inexplicable. Thus everything takes on an intensity and an hypertrophied sense of meaning. The magician finds the most conventionally ordinary things deeply weird and considers nothing impossible.

Nevertheless the magician needs to dance carefully on the edge of the abysses..........

Chapter 24

HERESY V

The Abysses

The so-called Oath of the Abyss wherein the adept vows to interpret every phenomena as a direct message from the ultimate reality to his or her self will indeed open several possible abysses, but to no constructive purpose.

Commentary 24

Forget all that Golden Dawn and Thelemic stuff about the Abyss and Crossing the Abyss. Three major pitfalls await the traveler on the short and dangerous path of magick. The initial exhilaration of accelerating into each may for a time, mask mounting failure in reality.

The Abyss of Paranoia pays initial dividends in self-importance, but, as this 'effective' paradigm takes hold, things will really start to go wrong in a big way, and enemies will fill the spaces you reserve for them.

The Abyss of Sophistry pays initial dividends in ease and leisure, but the more you imagine yourself innately and effortlessly magickal, the less effective you become. (See the following chapter.)

The Abyss of Obsession pays initial dividends in a hypertrophied feeling of meaningfulness. However, no insight can have universal application, and the areas it misses will eventually explode in your face.

To the diamond wisdom sutra of 'Enchant Long and Divine Short' we should perhaps add:

'Don't Invoke that which only merits Evocation.'

The magician only fully identifies with well formed gods, and then only for a period. Keep the demons in the triangle of Arte. Mistake not the demon Choronzon who hath single form, for the multiplicious Holy Guardian Angel who hath legions of names. Your 'real self' consists of many selfs.

Chapter 25

HERESY VI

Dropping the Wand

Does 'the power of the way you live' cause magick to occur effortlessly?

Do you use 'True Will' as an excuse to do nothing?

Do you think that even when things apparently go badly for you, your inborn spiritual wisdom and power have arranged an initiation for you, despite your conscious desire?

(They may well have, but how do you choose to interpret the message?)

Do you no longer need your instruments and the technical procedures of spells and servitors?

Have you declared yourself enlightened?

Commentary 25

Damn your weak philosophies; a pox and a pestilence upon your despicable sloth and arrogance.

Either give up now, tear off those adept's stripes that you once won and join the New-Agers, or pick up that wand and let's see half a dozen tight sigils launched with full gnosis before dawn.

Great wizards never exist in a state of masterly inactivity in imagined perfect worlds. Great wizards study, strive and conjure till they drop. They have much to do; the quest on which humanity has embarked has barely begun.

Those declaring themselves enlightened merely display their inability to imagine the extent of what they don't know.

Chapter 26

HERESY VII

Off-White Magick

The phrase Black Magician unfairly applies to anyone who has taken your lover or money by occult means. However, Self-Professed Black Magicians seem universally unable to fight, fuck, or even buy their way out of wet paper bags, despite fantasizing constantly about becoming powerful psychopaths. The high point in a career of ultimate evil — getting badly scratched whilst failing to strangle a cat, ha! ha! ha!

Those sanctimonious transcendentalists who profess themselves White Magicians never do anything unpleasant without the very best of spiritual reasons, but spend most of their careers casting ineffectual spells at imaginary evils to no effect. An averse pentagram scrawled on their doorsteps as a joke can keep one busy for several years.

Off-White magickians require no spiritual or demonic justification for their acts, and can take your lover or money without leaving you feeling bad about it.

Commentary 26

Such flippancy ill becomes Frater Stokastikos, who allied himselfs with the off-white tradition on account of its superior sense of humour.

Chapter 27

HERESY VIII

Magus Chase

The summary of a paradigm in a Word may please those who like simple slogans like THELEMA or CHAOS, but underneath it all a magickian basically issues the challenge "Follow Me", upon assumption of the role of magus within an order.

No stimulus to personal achievement can match the effects of a large body of people chasing you for blood.

No other motive for assuming the role of magus has nobility, but no honour attaches to those who will not retire when exhausted, or those who simply wait for their pursuers to lick their feet or crucify them.

The retired magus may take the role of Ipsissimus, applying the Treasures won in the race at will, and shouting encouragement and unwelcome criticism from the sidelines at those who failed to realize what they had signed up for.

Commentary 27

We shall mention no names …

… …*except our own.*

Yes we exited stage left soon after winning a slightly Pyrrhic victory in the Ice War.

Exhausted and with no fresh innovations to offer at the time, a sabbatical seemed like a good idea.

Yet the 15 year mid-career research leave did not provide a holiday but more of a mental assault course.

Finally Apophenia turned up and showed us the eight dimensional vorticitating hypersphere, so it all seems worth it.

Thus we revoked our Ipsissimus role, reverted to the role of ordinary Magus, and opened Arcanorium College.

We had fresh material and a new generation wanted to hear the initial material as well, plus we needed a Think Tank.

Chapter 28

HERESY IX

Astrology

Some star signs may seem more inclined to believe in astrology than others. In particular, those either born or nurtured with their Intellect in Faeces, make the best candidates.

We once met an astrologer in a cast, who had a perfectly rational reason for his broken leg.

Commentary 28

The pseudoscience of astrology has no place in magick.

Astrology has already died twice: once with the classical gods, and a second time after the Enlightenment. The complete failure of contemporary psychology to create anything other than a vocabulary of intellectual rubbish has encouraged astrology to resurface.

You can make money out of it easily.
You can get people into bed with it sometimes.
But otherwise, forget it.

Apparently all Capricorns with Uranus in direct opposition to their Sun act like opinionated contrarians and say things like this.

Thus we apologize for this inevitable and entirely predictable outburst.

Chapter 29

HERESY X

New-Ageism

I could love it: —
If dolphins had as much intelligence as cats,
And stopped trying to rescue sinking pieces of wood.
If crystals actually did something useful,
Other than grease the wheels of commerce.
If the Goddess had made animals taste less good,
So I didn't want to eat them.
If astrology could tell me anything,
Other than the trite and the obvious.
If whales could do something more impressive,
Than merely occupy a lot of space.
If corn circles came from enlightened aliens,
Rather than Wiltshire pranksters on cider.
If channellers could speak in hieroglyphics,
Instead of pop-psychological twaddle.
If sharing, caring, non-sexist men,
Could do anything useful in a crisis.

Commentary 29

The hippies of '68 broke the dress code and the sex code, stopped a major war, and created a healthy disrespect for all forms of authority. Mysticism and music functioned as enemies of the state in those days.

The starry-eyed idealists of today have submerged their critical faculties beneath a tidal wave of slop marketed by those old hippies who now sell a user-friendly dilution of their original enlightenment.

Well, we still seem to have some hardcore Chaoists left despite the sad loss of Robert Anton Wilson, and we have some new ones as well. The war against consensus reality continues.

Chapter 30

HERESY XI

Dog God

In domesticating the wolf
We have reduced the wild ideal
To grotesque parodies of ourselfs:
And so with our Gods.

Commentary 30

In the transmissible mental disease of god ownership, the victim acquires the megalomaniacal delusion that a being supposedly representing all of his most desirable characteristics actually rules
THE ENTIRE UNIVERSE

Conversely, in the acquired personality defect of dog ownership, the sufferers seek emotional solace in a creature specifically bred to exhibit all their own worst and most childish instincts. For example, easily-bought loyalty and fawning affection; cringing obedience, alternating with loud emotional outbursts; and the tendency to bite the defenseless from behind and then run away and defecate in public.

Dog owners prefer to play god to creatures like that, rather than address their own personal and social inadequacies.

Deus es Canis Inversus.

By some supreme twist of cosmic irony the Memsahib has chosen a huge beast exactly resembling the preceding picture, much against our protestations.

Living with a dog confirms everything one suspected about the moral, intellectual, spiritual and hygienic superiority of cats, (who now spend most of their time in my wing of the mansion).

Chapter 31

HERESY XII

The Antichrist

A vile abomination lurks in obscene luxury at Rome. Heir to an empire built on industrialized slaughter and bureaucracy without culture. Self-preservation at any price. The empire created a faith when its war machine failed, then hitched itself to any bloody imperialism to extend its power.

The Lords of Albion fought it for three centuries, and weakened but did not break it. Now, in desperation, it sends out its celibate minions to make the masses breed a Pyrrhic victory by sheer numbers. Self-preservation at any price.

Commentary 31

The Pauline Church originated from the publicity work of a grotesque misogynist fanatic who never met the obscure Jewish religious figure upon whose myth he founded a cult. At the Council of Nicaea, some centuries later, a desperate Roman emperor had the doctrines of the now diverse cults completely rewritten, redesigned and institutionalized, as an instrument of the state. After the collapse of the military and political wings of the empire, the religious arm began work on an empire of faith and fear.

The papacy has never hesitated to compromise its principles, or to burn and torture its opponents, or to ally itself with any bloody military adventure, recently including fascism, if it thought it could profit thereby. Its vast network of confessor-inquisitor-informers allowed it to survive as history's most grim and enduring conspiracy.

Like any organism that has successfully degenerated into a parasite, it now exists only to perpetuate itself at its host's expense. The cost so far? A hundred million killed, and history two centuries behind where it might have advanced to.

Since we wrote the above, a worldwide pedophilia scandal has engulfed the Catholic Church. Fear has probably kept the lid on this ghastly secret for centuries.

The Vatican continues to oppose humane measures to arrest the spread of HIV and excessive population growth.

Well why should they, it provides a good living for wicked old men, as with most religions.

Chapter 32

Heresy XIII

Fundamentalism

Do you feel:
Confused by post-modern life?
Unable to handle too much choice?
Fazed by information overload?
Uncertain about so many grey areas?
In need of some black & white certainties?
That you need some simple slogans to live by?
Intensely jealous of those who can handle modern life?
That you need something to hate?
Unhappy at flexible relative values?
That the past offers more promise than the future?
That the answer to your problems lies outside yourself?

Then much that now pours from the fundament of the major religions may interest you, schmuck.

Commentary 32

Just when we thought the antibiotic of rational enlightenment had finished off the worst of the theological viruses, along came virulent new strains to pollute and disease half the globe.

Ah well! Back to the lab.

We cannot allow the exhaustion of modernism to occasion a regression to pre-Enlightenment mediaeval world views.

Esoteric thought frequently acts as a precursor of entire cultural paradigms. Thus we must oppose the mediaevalism inherent in both fundamentalism and much of the New Age philosophy with a vibrant post-modernist Chaoism.

The situation with respect to fundamentalism seems to have worsened considerably since we wrote that, particularly in the third major monotheism. If the world slides further into ecological and economic problems we may expect worse to come.

Fundamentalism thrives on a vicious circle, as it worsens living conditions it drives more people more deeply into its own arms.

Chapter 33

HERESY XIV

Filthy Fun

Oral sex stands as an enduring monument to human ingenuity, but the given proximity of the organs of generation
and excretion explains much of human psychology and
philosophy.

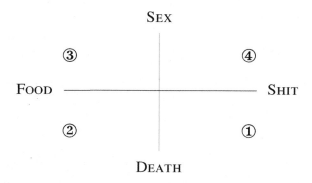

Commentary 33

①→ Hygiene Neurosis

②→ Dietary Neurosis, Vegetarianism, Anorexia etc.

③→ Overeating makes as poor a substitute for oral sex as smoking does for breast-feeding.

④→ Who has the most fun?
a. Those who demonize sex as unpleasantly dirty.
b. Those who demonize sex as pleasantly dirty.
c. Those who go the whole pig and reintegrate excretion into their sexual pleasures.

1. *Hygiene neurosis frequently leads to auto-immune diseases, don't forget Hormesis, we need a certain amount of dirt to keep our immune guards occupied, otherwise they may stage a palace revolt.*

2. *A significant proportion of people in rich countries now live in neurotic fear of their own diets and all the poisons they might contain. Haven't they got anything more important to concern themselves with?*

3. *Despite the hypersexualised popular culture we now 'enjoy' people today have less actual sex than they did a generation or so ago. (Overwork and stress apparently).*

4. *4b will do nicely thanks. Please don't bathe too frequently; it removes a lot of the sensuous enjoyment.*

Chapter 34

HERESY XV

Immortality

If we had Immortality,
We would desire Amnesia more.
As we consist entirely of our memories,
Immortality would have no point.

Paradox: Immortality for the human race would destroy the human race.

If you meet an immortalist, you know what to do; for your children, and for the sake of your children's children.

Commentary 34

Those who seek physical or 'spiritual' immortality have not thought the issue through.

Precisely what of themselves do they want to reincarnate, or to go to heaven, or to live forever?

As an eternally persistent memory would prove intolerable, we presume immortalists really desire some form of continuity of consciousness. However, continuity of consciousness arises only through a trick of memory. Herein lies the Paradox. After a few hundred years an immortalist would have either an intolerable burden of memories enough to dull any experience, or would have discarded or erased memories to the point where continuity of consciousness had become meaningless.

We have met those who aspired to immortalism in their middle years, yet curiously as they got older they seemed to turn against the idea. Maybe wisdom finally dawned.

Quality of life seems far more important than quantity.

Now that we seem to have overshot the human population carrying capacity of this planet we should bear that in mind.

Please reproduce responsibly, 95% of people result from accidents.

Chapter 35

HERESY XVI

An Unfashionable Hobby for many Wizards

With a simple wand and chalice you can perform the most chaotic conjuration of all—launch an entirely new person, and thus cheat death and throw bombs at the future.

We sometimes wonder if the obsession of mediaeval and renaissance sorcerers with creating various golems and homunculi arose from their distaste at the sheer chaos and unpredictability of the simpler method of creating little monsters.

People who act as various sorts of 'police' by profession, whether in the clergy, the actual police, or as academics, tend to have rebellious offspring.

Wizard's children often have a hard time finding something to rebel against, their parents having rebelled against just about everything.........

Commentary 35

We say that we have 'had' rather than that we have 'made' or 'created' a baby, as we cannot take responsibility for the unpredictability of the result. However, that very unpredictability supplies all of the delight and sorrow to the entire operation. How stupefyingly boring we would find clones of ourselves, if cloning becomes possible.

We do not wish to live forever. Our immortality sleeps soundly in a crib at the foot of the bed (sometimes!). We have reconfigured ourselves with a liberal dash of chaotic refreshment and renewal whilst still alive, and can now, with this jest, face death with equanimity.

Daughter 1. Now out of the nest and studying hard with a view to saving the planet as a professional ecologist.

Daughter 2. Showing promise but undecided about a career yet, perhaps a mathematician.

Stop at two. Your planet cannot support any more.

Chapter 36

HERESY XVII

Machine Enlightenment

Exercise One
Try to specify exactly and in detail any human functions that you do not believe a computer could carry out even in principle.

Exercise Two
Try to specify exactly and in detail what humans mean when they use the word 'spirituality'.

Commentary 36

Paradoxically an exact and detailed specification of any function will, in principle, allow a computer to perform it. Apologies for the trick question.

Only the unspecifiable remains, but let us not waste time with mystification; although we could write programs to produce plenty of it for fun and profit.

Any half sensible answer to the second exercise qualifies you as a fully enlightened master. Congratulations, you can now dress it up with the bullshit of your choice, and sell it.

We have an increasingly dynamic spiritual marketplace now due to an enhanced communications infrastructure.

Recycle your ontological waste products for hard cash!

Epistemological detritus fetches real money!

Try out your product online today!

Chapter 37

HERESY XVIII

Hazards

Commentary 37

For fun, gratuitous insult, as a humanitarian gesture, or to stimulate paranoia where appropriate, the magickian may print and display copies of these warning labels where appropriate. Standard international form requires Psi-Hazard warnings in black on a red background, and Mental Health Hazard warnings in black on an orange ground.[1]

Copyright waived on these decals.

Reproduce and attach to places of worship and political activity at will.

Alternatively simply have some labels run off which say 'For Entertainment Purposes Only' and stick them on items of religious literature and creationist publications.

---

[1] See *The Control of Noxious Substances from Eldritch Dimensions.* Ch.1497, para.89. *Health & Safety in the Temple.* Vol.146, ch.2. *Conjuration in the Workplace.* Vol.89, ch.3 & 4.

Chapter 38

HERESY XIX

Nothing

NOTHING IS TRUE
EVERYTHING IS PERMITTED

A decade on and the rest of the page remains blank for we still cannot find a single datum that remains true under all possible circumstances, nor evidence of the impossibility of anything under all possible circumstances.

But by all means have a go.......

Commentary 38

Attributed to Hassan I Sabbah. Note the multi-level oxy-morons, paradoxes and anontisms concealed within these statements.

The second statement celebrates the bottomless well of human ingenuity from which we have barely yet removed the lid. The flames of hell will doubtless lick out of it, scorching many, but only knowledge will awaken us from the nightmare of history.

We can find three obvious meanings to the first assertion:—
1) Nothing is true. Judge ideas by their relative usefulness, not against some imaginary finality.
2) Nothing Is ... true. Nothing exhibits being, but every-thing exhibits doing. Only the sluggishness of perception and thought creates the illusion of 'being'.
3) Nothing ... Is True. Life the universe and everything takes an extravagant journey from nothing to nothing. Let us, therefore, applaud the nothing and relish its extravagance.

3) *Amendment. We now suspect that it takes a journey from nowhere and nowhen in particular to other equally arbitrary locations. It did not come from a big bang and it will not end in a big crunch or entropy.*

Chapter 39

HERESY XX

A Chaoist Haiku

We believe in nothing:
The chaotic void within,
The chaotic void without.
Between nothing and nothing,
Let us conjure great doing.

Or

We believe in nothing:
But the chaotic creativity within,
The chaotic creativity without.
Nothing has being,
Let us conjure great doing.

Commentary 39

Any comment would mar the supreme simplicity of these haiku.

Contemplate their every nuance, use before ritual if desired.

Chapter 40

PHENOMENIZATION I

Time

Extrapolate your cosmological observations with classical relativistic theory and you will end up with such absurdities as the big bang and singularities in real time (and space), that negate the theory you started with.

Indeed, linear extrapolations make no large-scale sense in a universe that has spatial and temporal curvature.

Extrapolate with quantum chaotic theory and you will find that the 'big bang' occurred with equal probability in imaginary time at every point in the entirety of space that we now observe, to phenomenize the apparent mass and corresponding characteristic lightspeed of a universe finite but unbounded in both real time and space.

(?)

Still wondering what we meant by that.

And neither do any kind of causal extrapolations make much large scale sense in a universe with a lot of randomness and emergence in it?

Commentary 40

It should come as no surprise that we can observe structures within the universe having a greater age than classical relativistic theory predicts for the universe. You can after all travel any distance you like in excess of 24,000 miles around the finite but unbounded surface of the earth without falling off.

Similarly, you can travel for as long a time as you like around the four dimensional hyperspherical surface which constitutes this universe; although, as on earth, you cannot ever arrive at the same spacetime locus twice. The universe does not have any meaningful 'real' age, rather it has a temporal horizon of the order of 10^{10} years at all points of spacetime[1].

Future generations will look upon the question of the 'real' age of the universe with the same amusement with which we regard the mediaeval concern about the distance to the edge of the world.

---

[1] *Quite an accurate estimate at the time of writing. The calculations that have on many occasions over the last decade kept us up till the small hours, reveal an exact value of: 3.34 x 10^{17} seconds, plus or minus 15%, (about 11 billion years), and a corresponding hyperspherical antipode distance of 11 billion light years only.*

Chapter 41

PHENOMENIZATION II

Finite and Unbounded

Any finite and unbounded system of N apparent dimensions must actually have $N + N/2$ dimensions for closure. Consider the bending of a two dimensional sheet through a third dimension to create a finite and unbounded two dimensional spherical surface, for example.

Our universe consists of a four dimensional 'surface' comprising three dimensions of space and one of time, which achieves closure by bending through a two dimensional plane of imaginary time.

The plane of imaginary time thus lies orthogonal to our observed four dimensional 'surface'.

Wrong. Despite that space exhibits no preferred direction we labored for years under the illusion that because we needed extra time dimensions to explain quantum physics and magic then the 'extra' ones must somehow differ from what we conventionally conceive of as 'ordinary' time.

In fact time exhibits no preferred direction either; we merely define 'ordinary' time as whatever direction entropy appears to increase in. Clocks measure entropy, not time.

The three dimensions of space and the three dimensions of time achieve hyperspherical closure by curvature about a fourth dimension of space and a fourth dimension of time that appears to us as gravity.

Commentary 41

We concede that we have adopted a finite and unbounded universe as an act of faith in our own finite and unbounded imagination. Neuro-cosmology sets the limits of cosmology. However, this model at least has the virtue of supplying an answer to what lies 'outside' of the universe, and also what lies 'inside' of it.

Outside of the universe lies the ANA direction of future imaginary time which we may conceive of as having unlimited duration and information content, but no space, matter or energy. Inside the hyperspherical four dimensional 'surface' of the universe lies the KATA direction of imaginary time, of necessarily limited length. This asymmetry creates entropy and irreversibility, and an apparent arrow in real time, as the imaginary future contains more probabilities than the imaginary past.

Not entirely accurate in terms of our last decade of research. Three dimensional space and three dimensional time must each curve round a forth dimension to achieve a finite and unbounded configuration, so that makes eight dimensions in all. Moreover the fourth dimensions in which time and space lie embedded do not need to extend beyond the 3D spacetimes they contain. The wavelike pasts and futures thus have the same size in probability space.

Chapter 42

PHENOMENIZATION III

Thrice Upon a Time

Time has three dimensions, as does space. We cannot 'see' any of the time dimensions. A clock or calendar measures the 'passing' of time equally well in all three, just as a rule measures distances in any of the three spatial dimensions with equal ease.

Any apparent conceptual problems and mysteries associated with imaginary time disappear when you realize that you can only experience one immeasurably small instant consisting of all three temporal dimensions.

Classical and Relativistic calculations and expectations and common sense model past and future events along the dimension of ordinary time, whilst Magickal and Quantum calculations and expectations model probabilistic events on the plane of imaginary time orthogonal to ordinary time.

The above represents the original intuition which eventually led to a rigorous model with testable predictions.

Commentary 42

Two dimensions (a plane) of imaginary time provides a field in which many possible pasts and futures can exist as probabilities. (They also provide unlimited possible parallel universes to the present moment which cannot interact with each other or us.) A single dimension of imaginary time would only allow a single possible alternative event.

Three dimensions of time also arise from general considerations of symmetry, and can also supply an explanation of the properties of so-called fundamental particles, as we shall show in the hyperwarp chapters.

We seem to have got that right more or less by intuition. The mathematical confirmation however proved time consuming and very painful.

The guess about universes parallel to the present not interacting did not prove entirely accurate. Quantum superposition provides a clear example of phenomena with the same spatial coordinates having slightly different coordinates in orthogonal (sideways or 'imaginary') time.

Thus objects can apparently exist in two contradictory states simultaneously in the same place in space, but only because they exist in two slightly different 'places' in sideways time.

Chapter 43

PHENOMENIZATION IV

Imaginary Time

Tangible phenomena readily submit to measurement with so-called 'real' numbers. Thus, for example, we can have four apples, or minus four apples, if we happen to owe you four. Although time has little tangibility, we persist in measuring it with real numbers, even though for advanced scientific purposes we get better results by measuring time as an imaginary component of Minkowski space. Imaginary numbers appear as the square root of minus one, designated i, raised by some factor. Thus 1i, 23i and -127i represent imaginary numbers. As imaginary numbers measure intangible phenomena so well, less confusion would have arisen if mathematicians had called them 'intangible' instead.

Human perception and real numbers have tended to reduce the enormity of the whole of intangible time to a thin stream that we call real time. Consequently we have to use the rather weird mathematics of imaginary numbers if we wish to add the entirety of time back on to the convenient abstraction of so-called real time.

If we follow the Minkowski formalism of measuring time as imaginary space then 'imaginary' (sideways) time appears as a sort of PSEUDO-SPACE, a convenient location for quantum superpositions in the present to occur in, and a place to store all the multiverses of the past and future.

Wizards used to call this stuff 'Aether'

Commentary 43

Memory and limited imagination create so-called 'real' time by picking out a thin stream of dubious causality from the intangible immensity all around us.

Paradoxically, the convenient fiction of one dimensional 'real' time arises from our imagination, but the greater reality of the three dimensional temporal continuum has to bear the somewhat derisory label of 'imaginary'.

To anyone who has so completely missed the point of all this that he asketh: "Where lieth this imaginary time?" We reply: "Where lieth your real time; where lieth all those things that you might do tomorrow; where lieth all those things that you might have done yesterday; and where lieth both of those histories that contribute to the result of the double slit experiment in quantum optics."[1]

Stephen Hawking put his finger on this with the observation that entropy increases with time simply because we measure time in the direction in which entropy increases.

We define our direction of spatial travel as 'forward', similarly we normally define or direction of entropy increase as straight forward in linear time. We can see sideways in space but not in time, so we assume time has no sideways.

Thus we inhabit a tautological time of our own making.

---

[1] See any good advanced physics text and try to wriggle out of the discombobulating weirdness this entails.

Chapter 44

ANONTOLOGY I

Non-Being

For those who would take the short and dangerous path to Chaoist Anti-Ontology.

NOTHING HAS BEING

Adjust your mind; you have a serious fault in the linguistic programmes which structure your thought, which can halve your effective intelligence.

You might need a microscope or some particle physics equipment, but take a close look at anything and you will see that it constantly does things. Nothing just sits still in a state of being.

Everything has to keep moving and changing, if only by spinning internally, otherwise it wouldn't exist at all.

Exactly the same applies to humans and their minds.

You can never occupy a state of being.

Commentary 44

Attempt to describe 'being' and you can only actually describe doing.

We observe only 'doing'. We never observe 'being', 'existence' or 'essence'.

All phenomena, ourselfs included, consist of processes, not of 'things' performing processes. Language lets us down badly.

The false concept of 'being' acts as a word virus, scrambling our thoughts, for nothing consists of other than what it does. I think, therefore I think that I think, nothing more!

The word virus "I am" lies at the root of the mental diseases we call religion.

"I am that I am," said Moshe, speaking amongst himselfs as Jehova: thus making four mistakes simultaneously. You cannot achieve a state of 'being'. But you can achieve a surprising choice of states of doing.

Nothing 'is' anything else; although many events resemble or look like others. Every use of the word 'is' conceals a loss of information and a reinforcement of narrow views and prejudice.

Chapter 45

ANONTOLOGY II

The Antispells of Anonto

Chaoist thought does not imply merely thinking about particular unusual subjects. We do not intend to let you off so lightly. No, Chaoism demands a change in your basic vocabulary and technique of thought.

The word Grimoire, denoting a magickian's spellbook, derives from 'Grammar'; and the old word for magick, 'Grammarye', denoted conjurations with written and/or verbal spells.

Conventional grammar and language force concepts of 'being' and 'is'ness upon thought which then obstruct a clear view of reality. In the following two chapter micro-grimoire we present the basic anti-spells which can open thought to the real world of doing concealed behind the illusion of 'being'.

Commentary 45

Virtually all occidental spiritual masters will try and sell you the opposite theory of the reality of 'being' behind the illusion of doing.

Damn and blast the lot of them; let us have the courage to live and die without such comforting lies.

The particulate reality we experience only exists as an interference pattern for about ten to the minus forty-four seconds. Outside of that the universe consists of a vast wave pattern of probabilities extending about eleven billion years and eleven billion light years in any direction from any observer and participant.

We exist as a fleeting assemblage of particles in an ocean of aether of almost unimaginable, but not infinite size.

We have no choice but to do until our doing undoes us.

Anything else constitutes a lie which the credulous pay others to convince them of.

Another nice little earner for wicked old men.

Chapter 46

ANONTOLOGY III

Antispell One
The Ritual:—
To attack the spell of 'being' requires cunning. Use stealth and deviousness and paper, to assault the enemy's vulnerable extremities.

> **WRITE WITHOUT ANY TENSE**
> **OF THE VERB 'TO BE'**

Are, am, is, was, be: out demons out!

Verily, we have a terrible capacity to believe what we do rather than to do what we believe.

Hence ritual serves to change belief much more effectively than argument.

Forced conversion has proved surprisingly effective during the history of religious strife. Make people go through the motions and soon enough they adopt the corresponding beliefs to rationalize their behavior.

Of course exactly the same thing happens to a lot of people during their upbringing.

Real religious freedom also means freedom from religion; a secular society should prohibit the indoctrination of minors.

Commentary 46

The word virus of 'being' does not submit easily to defeat. Yet on paper, after some struggle, one may start to roll back the enemy. As it retreats you notice the enormity of the territory it once occupied. Vast areas of assumption dissolve into fresh and fluid thought. Every careless use of the words 'am', 'are', 'is', 'was', and 'be' reveals, upon correction, a wealth of ingrained assumptions and lost information content.

The archetypal mythological gods of magick usually took credit for inventing words and writing. Language structures perception, thought and belief. Language thus creates our reality, but language can suffer from viral attack and initiate disease in our thoughts. Beware of the enormous sorcery contained in these seemingly innocuous antispells: they can render you binocular in the land of the blind.

Try also reading out all the assertions of 'being' in anything you read. On encountering each example of 'am' or 'is' or 'was', try and see what shortcuts and assertions or questionable assumptions and equivalencies the writer has made.

Most religious mystical or philosophical writings dissolve into complete idiocy or mere matters of opinion upon such an analysis, and so do most political tracts.

Quantum physics makes no sense whatever in the language of 'being'. It makes no sense to say that a quantum 'is' a particle or 'is' a wave.

Chapter 47

ANONTOLOGY IV

Antispell Two
The Ritual:—
Having fought the virus of 'being' to a standstill on paper,
press the attack with the spoken word.

> **ELIMINATE BEING FROM SPEECH**

Precise speech begets precise thought.
(Though most people assume the obverse.)
Pause to rephrase when temptation occurs,
And risk the appearance of wisdom.
Rephrase all mistakes, if only mentally, afterwards.
Only extreme vigilance guarantees liberation from the negative magick of 'being'.

Group Ritual:—
In conversation agree to prompt each other to rephrase all inadvertent ananontic statements. Most of the nonsense that passes for philosophy, ideology and religion then miraculously disappears.

Commentary 47

Battle Plan

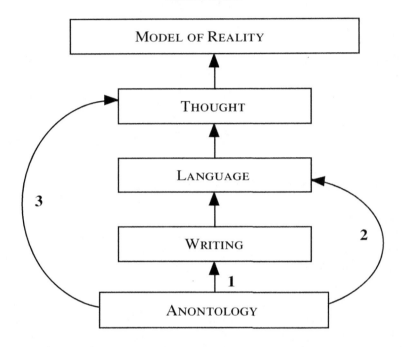

Antispells 1 and 2 should roll back the enemy and crumble the false model of reality.

However, if resistance stiffens, launch ANTISPELL THREE:

> ### ELIMINATE BEING FROM YOUR INTERNAL DIALOGUE

Chapter 48

PRACTICKS I

Three Conjurations More

As the Chaos Monasticism exercise of the Wand[1] proved so successful and popular, and no book on magick seems complete without offering something practical to challenge the aspiring magickian, we present operations of the other three classical elemental weapons.

We do not approve of the 'Crisis Magician' approach to The Great Work, few seem to get far by waiting for something to go wrong in their reality and then trying to patch it with magic.

Rather, as Mathers and Crowley recognized, magicians need to practice steadily like athletes and to make continual additions to their repertoire of techniques like scientists.

Thus oaths and resolutions to complete programs of magical activity have great value, as does keeping proper records.

Warning. A lot of the belief structure we inherit from our culture conspires against the quest for magic. You will have to struggle hard to complete such programs.

Persist!

---

[1] See our *Liber Kaos: The Psychonomicon.*

Commentary 48

As a spur to general proficiency and accomplishment, the current SAJALOM $\sqrt{1}°$ of the Pact hath agreed that Pact members who achieve a high standard of work with the operations of the four classical elemental weapons may present themselfs, their records, and their instruments, to a Magus of the Pact for possible accreditation as 'Master of Arms'.

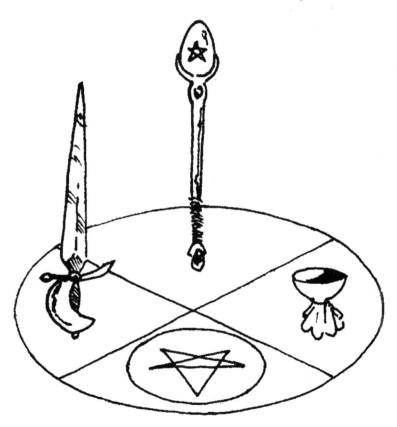

Chapter 49

PRACTICKS II

The Chaos Cyberzoo

Purpose: To evoke and use magickal servitors.

Daily Observances

The Lesser Observances
1) A proclamation of intent suitably worded.
2) Carry the pentacle at all times.
3) Visualisatory evocation of servitor's image(s) onto the pentacle, and despatch of servitors to some work of divination or enchantment twice in each twenty-four hour period.

The Greater Observances
1) All of the Lesser Observances.
2) Two further evocations, spaced equally around a twenty-four hour period.

The Extreme Observances
1) All of the Greater Observances.
2) The replacement of one of the visualisatory evocations with a full ritual evocation of the magickian's devising, to include a spoken address to the servitor etc. etc.

Commentary 49

The magickal operation of the Pentacle or disk (as with all the other instruments) should take place over a prearranged number of continuous days, after which the magickian may inscribe the instrument with a number marking the length and intensity of the work. Thus 213 represents thirteen days of Greater Observance, 33 shows three days Extreme, and so on.

The magickian may either evoke up to a maximum of four servitors which may have only astral shapes, or commit the entire operation to the creation and use of a multipurpose Eidolon having a previously prepared material basis.

Chapter 50

PRACTICKS III

The Jihad of Chaos

Purpose: To increase vitality and martial fervour and to attack offending forces.

Daily Observances

The Lesser Observances
1) A proclamation of Chaos Warriorhood, worded to taste.
2) Carry the magical dagger at all times.
3) Half an hour of hard physical exercise.
4) Half an hour's practice with martial arts and/or weapons.
5) Chaobolt one enemy target.

The Greater Observances
1) All of the Lesser Observances.
2) One half hour vigil with dagger and martial meditation before dawn.
3) Chaobolt a second enemy target.

The Extreme Observances
1) All of the Greater Observances.
2) A full red magick war ritual. (This may include one or both chaoboltings.)

Commentary 50

The magickian should, if possible, prepare the magical dagger by hand. Most conveniently, take the blade of a metal file and heat it glowing on a bed of charcoal whilst fanning the embers furiously, then allow slow cooling. Grind down to the shape of a blade with a second file. Reheat to cherry red and then quench to re-temper. Fashion and fit a guard and handle. Pass the used second file to a worthy colleague.

To chaobolt a suitable anti-chaotic institution or group, prepare a suitable sigil, visualize it astrally onto the dagger, and astrally hurl the resulting missile at the target. Alternatively, hurl the dagger physically at a symbolic image of the target, with full gnosis.

Chapter 51

Practicks IV

The Void of Chaos

Purpose: To seek inspiration or augury.

Daily Observances

The Lesser Observances
1) A proclamation of intent to access the chaotic void, suitably worded.
2) Bear the chalice concealed with you at all times, except during an exposure.
3) Perform a quiet Mass of Chaos B[1], omitting the circle dance and using distilled water as sacrament.
4) After the Mass, perform chalice gazing for half an hour.
5) Expose the chalice during the hours of sleep.

The Greater Observances
1) All of the Lesser Observances.
2) A further half hour of chalice gazing. Devote half of the gazing time to achieving voidness and half to visions.

The Extreme Observances
1) All of the Greater Observances.
2) A second Mass of Chaos B, preferably in the middle of a sleep period.
3) A further hour of chalice gazing.

---

[1] See our *Liber Null & Psychonaut*.

Commentary 51

This magickal operation of the chalice completes the four workings of the classical elemental weapons. The magickian should, if possible, create a chalice by hand; although this presents a challenge. When beating a disk of copper or silver, remember that both metals tend to harden with cold hammering and thus periodic heating can ease the task. Inscribe the chalice with the results of the work as for the wand, dagger and disk.

To perform a chalice exposure, leave the instrument outside the place of sleeping somewhere secure like a roof or a garden, and perform augury or meditation upon any contents found afterwards. To seek voidness or flow of vision, fill the chalice with dark liquid and gaze into it.

The SAJALOM died unexpectedly after a hectic year in office following our retirement, but not before achieving some astonishing accomplishments.

None has taken his place, the duties seemed too arduous. A council now administers the Pact.

The Jihad of Chaos now seems a rather strange turn of phrase, bearing in mind recent world events.

Nevertheless as the fifth aeon approaches and hangs in the balance, robust practices of this nature seem more necessary than ever.

Chapter 52

HYPERWARP 6D I

Prologue

In which we assert that particle physics has considerable relevance to magic.

As the 21st century begins, humanity finds itself in possession of a mass of confusing and seemingly arbitrary data about particle physics. What began as a quest to discover simplicity in the structure of reality has led to an embarrassing surfeit of subatomic bits and pieces, which exist for no obvious reason. As one physicist put it when finding yet another particle, "Who ordered that!?" The familiar proton, neutron, and electron of high school physics seemed to account for most things including chemistry, but in recent decades things became a whole lot weirder, so much so that the "standard theory" circum change of millennium can only manage a phenomenological approach which simply catalogues what happens without saying much about how or why.

Hyperwarp 6D asserts that spacetime singularities spinning in 6 dimensions (the familiar 3 of space and 3, rather than just 1, of time) can give a complete account of the existence and behaviour of all fundamental particles.

We advance this hypothesis in support of our contention that three dimensional time provides a better description of reality as a whole, and allows a more coherent model for explaining and advancing magic. We shall attempt to demonstrate this in the following 6 chapters.

Commentary 52

Background

Reality seems to work through two fundamentally different types of basic particle behaviour. Fermion (matter) particles with identical characteristics cannot occupy the same space, thus we cannot easily walk through brick walls. However any number of boson (force carrying) particles can pass through each other or occupy the same space, thus any number of people can see the same brick wall simultaneously from any number of angles. We shall address this profound mystery later on. Reality also exhibits a number of "fields" such as the electrostatic and gravitational, but in the H6D model these do not consist of particles. Firstly a consideration of fermions. Fermions come in just four basic varieties. Type 1 quarks have a unit of nuclear charge, (called the colour force) and a unit of electromagnetic (electroweak) charge. Type 2 quarks have a unit of nuclear charge and two of electromagnetic charge. Clusters of 3 quarks make up the familiar proton and neutron. Electrons have 3 units of electromagnetic charge, Neutrinos have no nuclear or electromagnetic charges, and we may, for the moment, regard them merely as bits of spin left over in nuclear reactions. So far so good, except that the proton and neutron do not seem as fundamental as we first thought. The weirdness really kicked in with the discovery that these four types of fermion all occur in *three* generations. Two much heavier versions of the electron called the muon and the tauon exist, and each type of quark has two much heavier relatives making *three* of each. Similarly *three* neutrinos exist, Each type of quark also has what we call one of *three* colours of nuclear charge. As all fermions have both particle and antiparticle manifestations, that all adds up to a rather large number. So has nature opted for a perversely baroque set of building bricks just for fun, or does some deeper principle explain her profligacy?

Chapter 53

HYPERWARP 6D II

Mysterious Fermions

First generation fermions make up all the stuff you see lying around on the average planet and all the stuff you can see with a telescope. To make the visible universe you only need first generation type 1 (down) quarks, type 2 (up) quarks, electrons, and some neutrinos to balance the books.

High energy cosmic rays produce muons when they hit the earth's atmosphere, but otherwise we only observe second and third generation fermions when we start smashing particles together in the extremely violent conditions inside particle accelerators. Under such conditions we also observe antifermions, which imply the possible existence of antimatter, but astronomers conclude with good reason that the universe does not contain any significant amount of antimatter; it seems very unlikely that anti-stars, anti-planets, or anti-aliens exist.

So why does reality have these apparently superfluous and unused behaviour patterns?

Commentary 53

Answer

We assert that even first generation fermion particles cannot work in less than 3 dimensional time. Higher generation fermions have to manifest as a consequence of 3 dimensional time, but they only manifest at high energies, which we do not normally observe. Magic also has to exist as a consequence of 3 dimensional time.

Following a brief digression to bring boson (force carrying) particles within the scope of this argument, we shall proceed to demonstrate the explanatory power of three dimensional time.

Many questioned the sanity of our quest to find evidence of three dimensional time in the physical universe. However we assert that only a universe based on 3D time will exhibit the behavior of ordinary matter that we observe.

Furthermore we assert that the peculiar bits of material reality we can observe like top quarks, tau-electrons, and Z-bosons, exist for precisely the same reason that the peculiar phenomena of magic occasionally appear.

And even furthermore we assert that magic forms a natural part of material reality. We inhabit a single awesomely complex reality which includes magical phenomena. Magical phenomena do not arise from some bizarre separate 'spiritual' reality, whatever that might mean.

Chapter 54

HYPERWARP 6D III

Mysterious Bosons

Bosons or "force carrying " particles carry energy between fermion or "matter" particles, In addition to the familiar "quanta" or photon wave/particles of light and electromagnetic radiation, two other types of boson called gluons and weak force bosons also exist.

Within H6D all bosons have a particle/antiparticle components and these components orbit about each other to produce the phenomenon of frequency and wavelength.

Specifically, photons have electromagnetic charge/anticharge components, gluons have colour/anticolour components, charged weak bosons have electron/antineutrino or positron/neutrino components and neutral weak bosons have components corresponding to electron/positron pairs.

The spacetime distortion induced by the spins of fundamental particles accounts for the existence of all fields, but accelerated masses may generate gravitons. General relativistic spacetime curvature by all forms of mass/energy continues to explain gravitational fields. Thus H6D finds no use for the hypothetical Higgs boson.

Still no Higgs boson at the time of writing. So far, so good.

Commentary 54

Quantum Weirdness

Three dimensional time has much to offer by way of explanation for the strange behaviour of fermion and boson particles at the quantum level. The phenomena of entanglement, non-locality, and probabilistic behaviour all have their roots in 3D time and the reversibility of time on the quantum scale. Consider Maxwell's equations of electromagnetism, the normally discarded "advanced wave" solutions, which apparently describe radiation going backwards in time, correspond exactly to the antiparticle components of bosons. Every little bit of light brings with it its own little piece of darkness to balance the books. This renders light (and bosons in general) intangible and invisible (except to an absorber), and able to interpenetrate itself.

Clearly we cannot quantise gravity because gravity varies continuously with the mass/energy spacetime distortion causing it. Rather we should consider "geometricating the quanta," as shown overleaf. Basically if we consider all the spins that a particle could have in 6 dimensions then, somewhat miraculously, we end up with precisely the set of experimentally observed particles, if we implement just a couple of simple rules.

Chapter 55

HYPERWARP 6D IV

Hyperspin Principles

1) If we define the spatial axis of a particles purely spatial spin as s1 then its spatial spin consists of a rotation of s2 and s3 about s1. (Notation s1/s2, s3), designated S.

2) Similarly a particle can have one purely temporal spin from the three possibilities t1/t2, t3 or t2/t1, t3 or t3/t1, t2. Such spins correspond to the three colours of the strong nuclear force, designated C.

3) Now if all 3 temporal spins have equal orthogonality to all spatial dimensions (don't try to visualise this at home folks), then this permits just six possible mixed spins.

4) The spins t1/s2, s3 & t2/s2, s3 & t3/s2, s3 correspond to the electromagnetic, or more properly the "electroweak" charge, designated E.

5) The spins s1/t2, t3 & s2/t2, t3 & s3/t2, t3 correspond to the particles generation, designated G.

6) All spins carry energy and subtend a spacetime distortion which we recognise as mass and gravitational field.

7) The colour and electroweak spins also subtend higher order spacetime distortions which we recognise as strong nuclear and electroweak fields.

8) All fundamental particles must have S and G spins to exist, but these may mask each other in non fundamental particles.

9) All the above spins can occur in left (-) or right (+) hand mode.

10) All fundamental particles must have either +3 or –3 or 0 spins with temporal axes.

11) C and E spins have temporal axes and thus change sign in temporal inversion, so antiparticles have opposite charges.

12) S and G spins have spatial axes and thus change sign in spatial inversion (change of direction), this leads to some astonishing conclusions, see Chapter 57.

Correction. Points 1-5 now seem to have expressed the Hyperwarp/Hyperspin hypothesis incorrectly, because they do not explain why they have the effect posited in point 6.

A better model arose from the consideration of the universe and all particles as vorticitating hyperspheres. In this new model the various axes of three dimensional space and three dimensional time rotate against the fourth curvature dimensions of space and time which relativity recognizes as gravity.

Otherwise the hypothesis remains largely unchanged.

Both fundamental particles and the universe as a whole have a spin or vorticitation whose angular velocity W, corresponds to:

$$W = \sqrt{2\pi G d}$$

where $d = \pi M / 2L^3$, *and where* $M/L = c^2/G$.

Commentary 55

Particle Types in the H6D Model

FERMIONS				BOSONS			
Neutrino				Graviton			
S	C	E	G	S	C	E	G
-1			1,2,3	&2			@1
Electron				Photon			
S	C	E	G	S	C	E	G
&1		-3	1,2,3	&2		@1	@1
Quark Type 1				Z Boson			
S	C	E	G	S	C	E	G
&1	1	-1	1,2,3	&2		@3	@1
Quark Type 2				W Boson			
S	C	E	G	S	C	E	G
&1	1	2	1,2,3	&2		&3	@1
				Gluon			
				S	C	E	G
				&2		@1	@1

KEY: & indicates plus or minus, @ indicates plus and minus in a condition of non-annihilatory cancellation.

And there you have it, QED, the manifestation of all fundamental particles explained as a consequence of the same 3D time that makes magic possible as well.

Note that antiparticles have opposite C and E spins to the particles shown, whilst antineutrinos have S+1 spins.

We shall examine the Hyperspin principles 10 and 12 in the following two chapters.

Chapter 56

HYPERWARP 6D V

Hyperspin Principle 10

The principle that fundamental particles must have either +3 or −3 or 0 spins with spatial axes allows only certain types of fundamental particle to exist, and these correspond to exactly the ones we can observe, but what physical meaning does it have?

Well in spatial terms no real object can have less than three dimensions and continue to exist spatially. Even an apparently two dimensional sheet of paper must actually have a finite thickness to exist in space at all. Something similar seems to apply to time.

Principle 10 also manifests in two other ways. The colour spins carry much more energy than the electroweak spins and so quarks always configure themselves to achieve an additional +3 or −3 or 0 colour spin state in baryon triplets or meson doublets. A third and somewhat weaker manifestation of the principle occurs in relation to the electroweak spin states in that only configurations with overall +3 or −3 or 0 electroweak spin states such as protons, antiprotons, and neutrons exhibit stability.

Commentary 56

Symmetry and Asymmetry

If time has the same sort of three dimensional symmetry as space, and all spins can have a positive or negative sign then how come the universe does not seem to consist of half matter and half antimatter? Furthermore, how come the universe seems to have undergone such profoundly asymmetric processes as the so called "Big Bang" and does it remain subject to such irreversible and asymmetric activities as Black Hole formation?

Well H6D does exhibit many of the symmetries of conventional theory, but as a consequence of Principle 12 it has a massive inbuilt asymmetry that gets rid of natural antimatter, black holes, and the big bang altogether.

At the time of writing nobody has observed such phenomena, although most physicists assume on purely theoretical grounds that black holes exist and that a big bang did occur.

The following chapter and its commentary contain assertions that conventional physics considers highly heretical, despite that little evidence exists to contradict them, and some data exists to support them.

As potentially testable predictions these assertions constitute possible experimental tests of the hypothesis of three dimensional time.

Consider the gauntlet thrown.

Chapter 57

HYPERWARP 6D VI

Heretical Predictions

Particles carrying C or E spins and charges can only annihilate against appropriate antiparticles. However because of the reversal of S and G spins with reversal of spatial direction, neutral particles can also annihilate against particles as well as against antiparticles.

Example: Neutrino (n), and antineutrino (a). S and G spins with respect to an s1 direction from left to right.

n> (S-1,G+1) <a (S-1,G-1)

a> (S+1,G+1) <n (S+1,G-1)

Thus neutrinos will give Z bosons against antineutrinos, but neutrinos against neutrinos (or antineutrinos against antineutrinos) will give photons.

Even more astonishingly neutrons should annihilate against neutrons, so long as the S spins match, and under appropriate conditions we should expect the reverse of this reaction to occur. You may well ask what happens to the colour spins of the quarks within the neutrons, well neutrons have no overall colour charge as they contain the colour charges called red, green, and blue, which collectively add up to zero, rather like + and − canceling.

H6D also suggests that whilst matter and antimatter particles generally have equal energy, nature may favour configurations where S spins configure anti-parallel to G spins, thus favouring left handed fermions, and hence favouring neutrinos over antineutrinos.

Commentary 57

Evidence and Controversy

1. Our star, the sun, does not seem to emit enough neutrinos to match its energy output. Do some neutrinos annihilate others before they get here?

2. Once or twice a day on average, an horrendous burst of high energy photons (gamma rays) hits our world. Fortunately the atmosphere stops nearly all of it. Such gamma bursts seem to come from events of staggering violence from beyond our galaxy. As heavy stars begin to collapse in on themselves towards the end of their lifetimes we know that the matter in them becomes compressed into a solid mass of neutrons. If at this point the neutrons start to annihilate each other then the whole thing would explode in a blizzard of gamma rays, and no black hole.

   The reverse of this process could occur in deep space where the photons hurtling around may slowly form new matter particles. Such a recycling of energy to matter would only have to occur at a rate of a single particle per cubic metre of space per several million years. Perhaps we inhabit a steady state universe after all.

3. If a mechanism exists to impede the progress of light across the universe, it will not have the effect of actually slowing light from lightspeed, it will merely remove some of its energy and make the light shift to a lower frequency. Now the observed redshift of light from distant sources constitutes the main evidence that the universe exploded from a big bang. It may have another explanation. The gravity of the universe redshifts the light all on its own.

Neutron-neutron annihilation, perhaps conducted inside a radio frequency linear accelerator, offers the possibility of direct mass to energy conversion!

Chapter 58

HYPERWARP 6D VII

Against Infinity

Whenever a calculation or a line of thought leads to some quantity having an infinite value then a mistake has occurred. Either an assumed infinity has become surreptitiously multiplied in, or an inadvertent division by zero has occurred. We cannot in principle observe any infinite quantity of anything, nor can any infinite quantity of anything actually exist without every quantity of everything having an infinite value, and if infinite quantities of everything exist, then the chances of such infinities canceling to give an even remotely comprehensible universe seem infinitely remote.

We mention this because at the turn of the millennium, conventional scientific thinking seems to have adopted an irrational belief in a number of assumed infinities. When even the infallible intellects of the Vatican declare that the big bang theory broadly accords with their own transcendental theories of Cosmo-genesis and eschatology, then evil sorcerer scientists such as ourselfs instinctively seek alternative luciferic viewpoints.

Hyperwarp 6D conveniently eliminates the infinities associated with big bang and with black holes and suggests instead a universe finite and unbounded in space and time and in thermodynamic behaviour.

Commentary 58

Finite and Unbounded

If time has three dimensions rather than just one as commonly assumed, then the universe can exist as a four dimensional "hyperspherical surface" closed by curvature about the other two dimensions. Such an hyperspherical surface will have no beginning or end in our perceived four dimensional spacetime. Although the surface itself would have only a finite extent in space and time we could never find an edge or boundary to it unless we somehow look "sideways" in time, As with travel round the surface of the earth, we can never encounter the same point in spacetime twice.

If the neutrons which form in superdense cosmic objects under the influence of gravity must eventually annihilate themselves in a titanic burst of energy as H6D predicts, and if this transmutation of matter to energy occurs in reverse in deep space, even at an almost imperceptible rate, then the universe cannot get stuck forever in sterile thermodynamic modes such as black holes or diffuse gases at equilibrium.

These intuitively derived conclusions still generally stand, and we have reinforced them with a mathematical analysis which shows that the hyperspherical universe must also vorticitate.

Vorticitation corresponds to a type of 'rotation' but in four dimensions rather than three, and at a mere 0.006 arcseconds per century it generally passes unnoticed whilst gently preventing the universe from imploding.

Chapter 59

ABOUT THE AUTHOR

(The Publishers Requested This)

The author values ideas above personality and thus, for example, prefers to read science fiction rather than soap opera.

The author experimented with mediocrity until the age of twenty-five and then decided that excellence offered better opportunities. The author still takes this view at forty-three, despite frequent exhaustion.[1]

The author chooses to maintain an antique and idiosyncratic code of chivalry, honor, and heroism in an era largely devoid of such things, just for the antinomian fun of it.

The author values uniqueness in an era of mass production and consumption, and values self-made, or at least hand-made, artifacts above all others.

The author captained the Magical Pact of the Illuminates of Thanateros for a decade and derived immense satisfaction from the progress made in the theory and practice of magic(k) during this period, but grew to despise the slavish imitation and treachery with which many mortals seek to advance themselves.

---

[1] *Now at 55 we adhere with fresh fury to this resolution.*

Commentary 59

'Only mediocrities fail to organize their time and material.'

– Wise words vouchsafed to us at age 15 by a Great Sage, but ignored for a decade. He certainly had the measure of us, and provoked us mightily with the assertion/challenge that 'You will never write, Carroll.'

(Our much revered English teacher, Old Bill Lawrence, now almost certainly deceased, thank you Sir.)

Magis Longa, Vita Brevis.

Choyofaque!

The author does not wish to burden others with the task of emulating the multiple eccentricities of his lifestyle, sexuality, dress, hairstyle, lip topiary, or manicure. We leave that to the Aleister Crowleys of this world. Thus, without photographs or style tips we arrive at

THE END

Chapter 60

EPILOGUE

After many years of struggle we wrote this book in frenzy to the accompaniment of thunderous music, partly for the exhilaration of doing so, and partly in the hope of reaching a few persons of like mind. The Magical Pact of The Illuminates of Thanateros already contains a number of like minds. To contact the Pact search the Internet and look there also for Chaos Magic, the current consists of rapidly mutating alliances and paradigms and addresses as you might expect.

We personally maintain a site at:

www.specularium.org

For the largely unforeseeable future.

We have a zillion things to do for now, so don't expect another book till well into the twenty zeroes.

(08/08/08 marks the date, we usually keep our word)

We will pass on all reasonable correspondence to Pact agents if requested, except for particularly pertinent comments on the Hyperwarp hypothesis.

Phew, finished a book without using a single "are" "is" "was" or "be" of our own. Out Demons Out!

Pete.

Chapter 61

ADDENDUM

May as well finish on a song: —

'Onward Chaos Soldiers'

Onward, Chaos soldiers, marching off to war,
With the Star Octaris going on before.
We fight for the Aeon, and against its foe;
Forward into battle see our armies go!

Refrain

*Onward, Chaos soldiers, marching off to war,
With the Star Octaris going on before.*

From the star Octaris see the Fundoes flee;
On then, Chaos soldiers, on to victory!
Hell's foundations quiver at our mighty spells;
Wizards lift your voices, loud with rebel yells.

Refrain

As a mighty army moves the Wizard horde;
Spells and sigils flying, Baphomet adored.
We are sub divided, multiple are we,
One in hope and Catmas, one in clarity.

Refrain

What the saints established nothing I hold true.
What the saints believèd, don't believe that too.
Everything permitted, we the faith will hold,
Theories faiths and paradigms, in destruction rolled.

Refrain

Crowns and thrones may perish, aeons wax and wane,
But the church of Chaos constant will remain.
Tales of hell can never 'gainst this church prevail;
We made our own promise, and that may not fail.

Refrain

Onward then, ye people, join our happy throng,
Blend with ours your voices in triumphant song.
Glory, laughs and honor to the great mythos,
Through the many aeons comes almighty Chaos.

Refrain

Commentary 61

A little light blasphemy set to a stirring tune to fortify those engaged with Jihad of Chaos in these' interesting times'.

The Fifth Aeon hangs in the balance, the world situation looks pretty grim, with too many of us with too many antique ideas on a planet creaking under the strain.

Dystopia becons but we could try something else.

Key:

The star Octaris = the eight rayed star of Chaos.

Fundoes = Fundamentalists of all pursuasions.

Baphomet ~ here represents the Biosphere.

Catmas = the opposite of Dogmas.

FURTHER ITEMS OF INTEREST

Liber Null & Psychonaut, Peter J. Carroll, Samuel Weiser Inc., 1987.

Liber Kaos, Peter J. Carroll, Samuel Weiser Inc., 1992.

Prime Chaos: Adventures in Chaos Magic, Phil Hine, The Original Falcon Press, Tempe, AZ, 2009.

Condensed Chaos: An Introduction to Chaos Magic, Phil Hine, The Original Falcon Press, Tempe, AZ, 2010.

Uncle Ramsey's Little Book of Demons. Ramsey Dukes. Aeon Books, 2005.

The Apophenion,—A Chaos Magic Paradigm. Peter J. Carroll. Mandrake Press, 2008. (1st Edition 08/08/08).

CEREMONIAL MAGIC & THE POWER OF EVOCATION

by Joseph C. Lisiewski, Ph.D.

Introduced by Christopher Hyatt, Ph.D. & S. Jason Black

Ceremonial Magic lays bare the simplest of Grimoires, the Heptameron of Peter de Abano. Its Magical Axioms, extensive Commentaries, copious notes, and personal instructions to the reader make this a resource that no serious student of Magic can afford to be without. It is all here, as in no other Grimoire. Use its instructions and the world of evocation and personal gratification are well within your grasp!

ISRAEL REGARDIE & THE PHILOSOPHER'S STONE

by Joseph C. Lisiewski, Ph.D.

Introduced by. Mark Stavish

Dr. Lisiewski delves into the hitherto unknown role Israel Regardie played in the world of Practical Laboratory Alchemy: not the world of idle speculation and so-called "inner alchemy," but the realm of the test tube and the Soxhlet Extractor. For the first time Dr. Regardie's private alchemical experiments are revealed as is his intense interaction with Frater Albertus of the Paracelsus Research Society and later, with the author himself.

KABBALISTIC CYCLES & THE MASTERY OF LIFE

by Joseph C. Lisiewski, Ph.D.

Foreword by Christopher S. Hyatt, Ph.D.

This groundbreaking book reveals a new system of occult cycles that gives you complete Control over your own life. The Kabbalistic Cycles System explains heretofore hidden universal laws known to but a few. The knowledge of these strange cycles—and the detailed, step-by-step explanation of their derivation and use—will place you light years beyond those who would maintain a stranglehold over you.

KABBALISTIC HANDBOOK FOR THE PRACTICING MAGICIAN

by Joseph C. Lisiewski, Ph.D.

Foreword by Christopher S. Hyatt, Ph.D.

For the practicing Magician, there is no more crucial working knowledge than the Kabbalah. This complex structure serves as the backdrop against which the magician's thoughts, ideas, ritual and ceremonial work are placed, and is the archetype which breathes life into secret occult practices. Yet, none of the numerous books on 'Qabalah' give those 'on-the-spot' attributions, correspondences and key concepts in a 'user-friendly' style. Until now.

URBAN VOODOO
A Beginner's Guide to
Afro-Caribbean Magic
by Christopher S. Hyatt, Ph.D. and S. Jason Black

Voodoo, Santeria and Macumba as practiced today in cities throughout the Western world. Includes descriptions of the phenomena triggered by Voodoo practice, divination techniques, spells and a method of self-initiation. Illustrated.

PACTS WITH THE DEVIL
A Chronicle of Sex, Blasphemy &
Liberation
by Christopher S. Hyatt, Ph.D. and S. Jason Black

Braving the new Witchcraft Panic that is sweeping America, *Pacts With The Devil* places the Western magical tradition and the Western psyche in perspective. Contains a detailed history of European 'Black Magic' and includes new editions of 17th and 18th century Grimoires with detailed instruction for their use. Extensively illustrated.

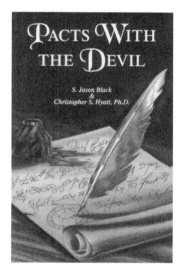

THE *Original* FALCON PRESS

Invites You to Visit Our Website:
http://originalfalcon.com

At our website you can:

- Browse the online catalog of all of our great titles
- Find out what's available and what's out of stock
- Get special discounts
- Order our titles through our secure online server
- Find products not available anywhere else including:
    - One of a kind and limited availability products
    - Special packages
    - Special pricing
- Get free gifts
- Join our email list for advance notice of New Releases and Special Offers
- Find out about book signings and author events
- Send email to our authors
- Read excerpts of many of our titles
- Find links to our authors' websites
- Discover links to other weird and wonderful sites
- And much, much more

Get online today at http://originalfalcon.com

Printed in Great Britain
by Amazon

41532458R00078